A Tricky
Sleepover

By Meg Greve

Illustrated by Sarah Lawrence

D1119732

Rourke
Educational Media
rourkeeducationalmedia.com

www.rourkeeducationalmedia.com

Edited by: Keli Sipperley
Cover layout by: Renee Brady
Interior layout by: Jen Thomas
Cover and Interior Illustrations by: Sarah Lawrence

Library of Congress PCN Data

A Tricky Sleepover / Meg Greve
(Rourke's Beginning Chapter Books)
ISBN (hard cover)(alk. paper) 978-1-63430-368-2
ISBN (soft cover) 978-1-63430-468-9
ISBN (e-Book) 978-1-63430-564-8
Library of Congress Control Number: 2015933725

Printed in the United States of America,
North Mankato, Minnesota

Dear Parents and Teachers:

Realistic fiction is ideal for readers transitioning from picture books to chapter books. In Rourke's Beginning Chapter Books, young readers will meet characters that are just like them. They will be drawn in by the familiar settings of school and home and the familiar themes of sports, friendship, feelings, and family. Young readers will relate to the characters as they experience the ups and downs of growing up. At this level, making connections with characters is key to developing reading comprehension.

Rourke's Beginning Chapter Books offer simple narratives organized into short chapters with some illustrations to support transitional readers. The short, simple sentences help readers build the needed stamina to conquer longer chapter books.

Whether young readers are reading the books independently or you are reading with them, engaging with them after they have read the book is still important. We've included several activities at the end of each book to make this both fun and educational.

By exposing young readers to beginning chapter books, you are setting them up to succeed in reading!

Enjoy,
Rourke Educational Media

Table of Contents

Chapter One

Where Is It?

"Jasmine! You got some mail!" Jasmine's mom yelled. Jasmine raced down the stairs.

Could this be it? Jasmine wondered. *Did I finally get the sleepover invitation from Kayla that everyone has been talking about?*

She tore open the envelope.

Ugh. It was just another summer camp brochure. Why didn't she get the invitation yet? Kayla let her sit with her and her friends at lunch the other day. She even shared her chips. Jasmine was sure she would be invited. She bit her lip and tried not to cry.

"Who is it from?" her mom asked.

"Camp Summerfun. Big deal." Jasmine shrugged.

"Do you want to go this summer?"

"I don't care," Jasmine said quietly.

"What is the matter?" Jasmine's mother looked worried.

"Nothing," Jasmine said. She sighed loudly and trudged back up the stairs.

Jasmine went to her room and threw herself on the bed. She was sure she would be the only girl at Walker Elementary who wouldn't be invited to the best sleepover ever. All of the girls were talking about it on the playground yesterday. Jasmine was so confused. Why wouldn't Kayla invite her? Jasmine always made sure she was nice to

Kayla and her friends. She hated feeling left out.

The next day when she got on the bus, there was an open seat next to her friend Annie. Jasmine plopped down next to her.

"Did you get an invitation to Kayla's party?" Jasmine asked.

"Yes! I got it in the mail yesterday! Aren't you excited? Our first sleepover ever and it's at Kayla's house! I heard her house has a room just for watching movies, and a room just for wrapping gifts!"

Jasmine slumped down in her seat. "I would be excited if I had gotten an invitation," she said, hiding her face behind her long, curly hair.

"What do you mean?" Annie said.

"I mean she didn't invite me," Jasmine said sadly.

"Oh, I am sure you will get it today. Maybe the invitation got lost," Annie said, patting her arm.

"I don't know what I will do if I don't get invited," Jasmine said. Her stomach was in knots. She pulled her hair out of her face and twisted it into a braid.

"Don't worry. If you don't get invited, then I won't go. You're my best friend." Annie gave Jasmine a little hug. "You know how to do the greatest braids! Your hair looks so pretty!"

Jasmine smiled at Annie and felt lucky to have such a great friend.

Chapter Two

The Invitation

Jasmine walked slowly through the hallways to her classroom. Some kids bumped into her, rushing to class before the morning bell rung. She saw a group of girls standing around Kayla, giggling and talking excitedly. She was sure they were talking about the sleepover on Friday. Jasmine never felt so terrible in her life.

"Jasmine! Jasmine!" someone shouted.

Jasmine turned to see Kayla waving something at her. She left her group of friends and rushed over to Jasmine.

"My mom just got this back in the mail. I think I had your address wrong. Will you come to my sleepover?" Kayla handed Jasmine an envelope. There was a stamp on it that said "Addressee Unknown."

Jasmine's heart raced with excitement.

"Yes! Thank you, Kayla!" She took the envelope and Kayla skipped back to her group of friends. Kayla's hair was long and always tied up in a ponytail. She twirled it and said something that made them all laugh. Jasmine hurried to class to tell Annie the good news.

Annie squealed with delight when Jasmine showed her the invitation. Both girls begged since they were in first grade to be allowed to have sleepovers. Their parents told them they had to wait until second grade. This was their chance!

Jasmine was so happy. But a new flutter in her stomach started as she counted the number of days until the party. What would she wear? Did Kayla and her friends sleep with dolls or stuffed animals? Jasmine had a favorite doll. She couldn't sleep without it. What if they don't? Would they think she was a baby?

Jasmine ran straight home as fast she

could from the bus stop that afternoon. She
burst through the front door, out of breath
and jumping up and down excitedly.

"Mom! Mom! I got invited to a sleepover!
Can I go? Please? Please?" Jasmine yelled.

Jasmine's mom came out of her office.
She was talking on the phone and held
her finger up at Jasmine to wait. Jasmine
bounced up and down, her braid swinging
wildly, until her mom finally said goodbye
to the person on the phone.

"What is this about a sleepover?" her mother asked. She seemed distracted about work and kept the phone to her ear.

"Kayla, a girl in my class, is having a sleepover and she invited ME!" Jasmine squealed. "And Annie can go too. And we have always wanted to have a sleepover. And I really want to go. Please?" Jasmine's words came tumbling out so fast, she sounded like she was on fast-forward.

Her mom laughed and kissed the top of her head.

"I guess you can. Do you think you can stay the whole night? This is a really big deal," her mom said. "Remember when you tried to sleep at Grandma's house? I had to come and get you at ten 10 o'clock at night because you were afraid."

"I can. I can! Thank you, Mom! I am going to call Annie!" Jasmine said.

Jasmine and Annie chatted happily about what they would wear, what they would bring, and which doll they would hide in their pillowcases. They decided they wouldn't tell anyone about needing their dolls to sleep. Jasmine was sure if she had her doll, she would be able to last the whole night.

Chapter Three

Secrets and Decisions

The long wait was almost over. The sleepover was the next night. Jasmine and Annie talked about nothing else since they both got their invitations.

Jasmine wound her hair in a special braid that morning. She couldn't stop smiling. When she got to school, she saw Kayla and her friends standing in a circle, laughing and whispering to one another. When Jasmine walked up to them, they stopped talking.

"Hi everyone," Jasmine said, smiling shyly at the group. "I am really excited about your party tomorrow night, Kayla!"

"Me too," Kayla said. "We have lots of surprises planned." Kayla's perfectly smooth ponytail was arranged over her shoulder. Jasmine looked at it wishing her hair would do the same. She was sure her hair was sticking up out of her braid all over the place.

"Like what?" Jasmine asked. All of the girls in the group were covering their mouths and giggling. Jasmine could feel her heart thudding in her chest. She tried to press down her hair. She thought for sure it was escaping from its twists and ties.

"Oh, you'll see," Kayla said in a sing-song voice. She walked away with the other girls, giggling and whispering to one another.

I wonder what that was all about, Jasmine thought. My hair must look really weird. She felt a familiar flutter of nervousness in her stomach.

Later that day, while Jasmine was in the library, she heard some girls whispering in another row. The voices sounded familiar to Jasmine. "I heard Annie and Jasmine haven't even been on a sleepover. I can't wait to teach them a couple of tricks! It will be so fun. Did you see Jasmine's hair today?" The two girls giggled as they walked down the row. Jasmine peeked through the shelf. It was Kayla and one of her friends!

Jasmine slowly unwound her braid. Jasmine didn't know what to do. Was Kayla planning on playing tricks on her and Annie? She was so angry. She was really looking forward to having a sleepover. Should she tell Annie? Maybe Kayla really didn't mean it. She walked back to class, thinking about what she'd heard.

Chapter Four

The Paint Trick

When Jasmine got back to class, she noticed a couple of boys standing near Kayla's desk. They had poured paint on her chair.

"Don't tell. Let's see what happens!" Tommy said.

Tommy and the boys high-fived each other, sat down, and tried to look bored.

Ha! Jasmine thought. Now Kayla will know what it feels like to have a trick played on her! She smiled sweetly and watched while Kayla sat down in her chair.

"AAAHH!" Kayla screeched. "Someone poured paint on my chair! My skirt is ruined!"

The boys erupted with laughter. Mr. Garcia, their art teacher, sent them to the

principal's office. Kayla hid her face as she cried.

Jasmine thought the trick the boys played on Kayla would be so funny. She thought it would make her feel so much better after what she overheard in the library. But now, all of a sudden, she didn't feel very well. Kayla seemed really upset and hurt that the boys would be so mean to her.

Maybe I should have warned Kayla about the paint, she thought.

Jasmine asked Mr. Garcia if she could go help Kayla get cleaned up. He let her take Kayla to the bathroom. Kayla was sobbing and her skirt was a mess. This only made Jasmine feel worse. Her feelings were so hurt by what she heard, she didn't think about how Kayla might feel to have a trick played on her.

Jasmine decided not to say anything to Kayla. She helped her get washed up. They walked to the office together so Kayla could call her mom to bring her some clean clothes.

"Thanks for helping me, Jasmine," Kayla said. "I am so glad we are becoming friends."

"Me too," Jasmine mumbled. Her stomach felt tied up in triple-knots.

Chapter Five

The Whole Truth...
Or Is It?

When Jasmine saw Annie on the bus after school, she told her all about what happened in art class. Annie's eyes opened wide and she let out a small gasp.

"Why wouldn't you tell her about the paint?" Annie asked.

"I overheard Kayla and the other girls in the library. I think they are planning to play tricks on us at the sleepover. They were also talking about my hair," Jasmine said. She felt both mad and ashamed at the same time.

"Why would they be so mean?" Annie said. "We just want to be their friends. Should we still go to the sleepover?"

"I think we should. But we should be prepared. If they want to play tricks on us, then we should be ready with our own!" Jasmine said.

The girls spent the rest of the bus ride making a plan. Neither wanted to tell the other, but they both had a very uneasy feeling about what they came up with.

When Jasmine got home, she plodded up the stairs. She wanted to curl up in a ball under her bed and hide. She never felt so unhappy. She didn't know what to do to make everything better. As she packed for the sleepover, she hid what they would need to play tricks on the other girls. Instead of feeling excited, Jasmine wanted to cry.

She didn't eat much that evening. After dinner, Jasmine's mom knocked on her bedroom door.

"I got some new clothes for you for the sleepover. I know this is a big deal for you," she said, handing Jasmine a bag with a skirt and matching shirt inside.

Jasmine thanked her, but she couldn't look her in the eye.

"What's the matter, honey?" her mom asked. Jasmine didn't want to tell her what happened, but the whole story came tumbling out of her mouth anyway.

Jasmine's mom hugged her tight and wiped away her tears.

"It is a good thing you helped Kayla clean up. But I think you owe her an apology," she said gently.

"Why do I owe her an apology? She was the one planning to play tricks on us," Jasmine said. She sniffled and wiped her nose on her sleeve.

"Are you sure you heard what you think you heard?" her mom asked.

"Of course I am sure," Jasmine said in a quivering voice.

It bothered her that her mother was questioning what the girls said. Jasmine was sure she heard them correctly. Or was she?

Chapter Six

A Change of Plans

The next morning, Jasmine saw Annie on the bus. She waved to Jasmine and moved over so she could sit down.

"Are you ready for the sleepover?" Jasmine asked.

"I guess," Annie said quietly. She had a funny look on her face.

"What's wrong?" Jasmine asked.

"I don't know, I just think maybe we should ask Kayla about what you heard yesterday. She seems so nice and really excited to have us over," Annie said. She clasped her hands between her knees and let out a deep breath.

Jasmine sat back in the seat and let out a big breath too. She didn't really want to go through with their plan. This was why she liked Annie so much. Annie wasn't afraid to be honest and share her feelings.

"I think you are right," Jasmine said. "Let's just forget our plan. I have a better one. Come over before the sleepover and I will braid our hair."

Chapter Seven

The Sleepover

Annie and Jasmine gave each other a quick hug before ringing Kayla's doorbell. Seconds later, the doorway was filled with smiling faces.

"Hi Jasmine and Annie! Come in! Come in!" The girls practically fell into the house as the girls pulled them inside.

Kayla's house was huge. She had a room with big comfy chairs and pillows and the biggest TV Jasmine had ever seen.

Kayla's mom said hello and her little brother pounded his chest and made ape noises. Everyone laughed and her mom shooed him out of the room. He stuck his tongue out at everyone on the way out.

"Boys," Kayla said, rolling her eyes.

"Jasmine and Annie, your hair looks so

pretty!" Kayla said. She looked really happy to see them.

The girls ate pizza, told funny stories, and watched a movie. Still, Jasmine and Annie didn't quite feel comfortable. Even though everyone seemed so nice, they were nervous about the tricks they might play on them.

"Okay girls, I have got some tricks up my sleeve for you!" Kayla said, jumping up from the pile of sleeping bags they'd been lounging on. "Come on, follow me!"

Jasmine and Annie glanced at each other. Annie bit her lip and shrugged. Jasmine took a deep breath, then followed Kayla and the others into the bathroom.

"It's time to do makeovers!" Kayla said. She pulled a comb, a curling iron, and some ribbons from the cabinet.

Kayla started to braid her best friend Maya's hair.

"Ouch! Stop it, Kayla! My hair looks terrible!" Maya said. It was true. Her hair was a frizzy, floppy mess. Jasmine tried not to giggle. She realized this was her chance.

"Hey, Maya, I know how to braid. Can I try?" Jasmine asked.

"Please do," Maya said. "Anything has to be better than this mess!" She laughed and stuck out her tongue at Kayla. Kayla stuck her tongue out at Maya.

Jasmine brushed Maya's hair, then weaved the strands into a complicated braid. Maya gasped when she looked at it in the mirror.

"This is awesome!" she squealed.

Everyone wanted Jasmine to do their hair. Annie helped Jasmine by organizing all of the styling tools. Then they painted their nails and tried on Kayla's mom's shoes. They played music and put on a fashion show.

When Kayla went into the kitchen to get drinks and snacks, Jasmine followed her. Her heart was pounding.

"I have a present for you," she said. Her voice sounded wobbly. She handed Kayla a bag.

Annie walked into the kitchen as Kayla

took the bag. She looked puzzled.

"No Jasmine! Don't do it!" Annie said.

"It's okay, Annie. I think you will like this better than our first plan," Jasmine said. She smiled at both of them.

Kayla opened the bag and pulled out the new skirt from Jasmine's mom.

"Oh wow! A new skirt! Thank you so much! But why did you get me a present? It's not my birthday!"

"I knew the boys put the paint on your

chair before you sat down," Jasmine said. She looked down at the floor then back up at Kayla.

Kayla's mouth opened, then shut again. She was quiet for a second.

"Why didn't you tell me?" she said. Her eyes looked watery.

"Because I heard you say you were going to play tricks on Annie and me at your sleepover. And I heard you talking about my hair. I was so mad at you that I decided to let you see how it felt to have someone be mean to you," Jasmine said. She twisted her braid nervously. "But I didn't realize how badly you might feel. I am really sorry Kayla," Jasmine's voice trailed off to a whisper. Her throat felt funny. Annie squeezed her hand.

"We didn't say we were going to play tricks on you. What I meant was that we were going to teach you fun sleepover games and how to curl your hair and stuff," Kayla said. "Why would I play tricks on you?"

Jasmine didn't know what to say. She was

so embarrassed that she misjudged Kayla. Especially since she wanted to be her friend!

"I am really sorry," Jasmine said again. "I should have asked you about what I heard. I was really looking forward to being your friend."

Jasmine thought Kayla might ask her to leave the sleepover. Instead, Kayla gave her a hug.

"I guess I can understand how you might have misunderstood. Next time, ask me!" Kayla said. "Now let's watch the rest of the movie!"

"You forgive me?" Jasmine said.

"Of course I do!" Kayla said. "Isn't that what friends are for?"

She grabbed Kayla and Annie's hands and jumped up and down. The girls' laughter brought the rest of the party to the kitchen.

"Everyone, I have a confession to make," Kayla said. Her face became very serious. Jasmine and the rest of the girls looked at her and waited.

Kayla reached into a cabinet and pulled out a tattered pink doll.

"This is MooMoo. I've had her since I was a baby. And I can't sleep without her," Kayla held her head up high and waited. No one said anything for a few seconds.

"Why do you keep her in the kitchen cabinet?" Maya giggled.

"Because I was hiding her for the party, silly," Kayla said.

Jasmine and Annie slipped out of the kitchen and came back with their own dolls. They held them up so the girls could see them.

Then the rest of the girls went and got the dolls they'd brought along. They sat at the table and talked about terrible nights when they'd tried to sleep without them. Jasmine knew she would be just fine when she climbed into her sleeping bag later, surrounded by friends.

"This is the best sleepover ever!" Jasmine said.

Reflection

Dear Diary,

When I think about this sleepover, I get so happy! Even about all the bad feelings before the party. I know that sounds so weird! It taught me that I should be proud of myself and what I can do. Sometimes you get invited to parties and sometimes you don't. That's okay. The most important thing is to always treat people nicely. The way you want them to treat you! That is much easier to say than to do sometimes. I also learned that asking for forgiveness is really hard. It made me feel so much better, though.

XO,
Jasmine

Discussion Questions

1. Why did Jasmine feel like Kayla might not like her?

2. What reasons does Jasmine give to want to go to the sleepover? Do you think those are good reasons? Why or why not?

3. How do you think Jasmine should have handled what she heard in the library?

4. How does Annie help Jasmine change her mind about the tricks they wanted to play at the sleepover?

5. Would you have forgiven Kayla? Why or why not?

Vocabulary

Look at the words in the list below. How are they used in the story? Can you write a sentence for each of the words to show you know what the word means?

apologized
apology
brochure
complicated
glaring
miserable
misunderstood
realize

Writing Prompt

Write a letter to Jasmine and tell her how she should have handled her tricky sleepover problem. Should she have let Kayla sit down in the chair? What could she have done instead?

Q & A with Author Meg Greve

Do you remember any bad sleepovers you had as a child?

I do remember one. My friends and I decided to cut my hair. That was a HUGE mistake! It looked awful, my friend's mom was really mad, and I had to have my hair cut really short to fix the problem! It didn't grow out for a year!

Do you have a daughter of your own? Did she have any sleepover problems?
I do have one daughter. She liked having sleepovers. I remember lots of times when she and her friends would come over, make a huge mess, and go to bed too late. Moms really don't enjoy sleepovers as much as their kids do!

Plan a sleep-under!

A sleep-under is a great party for kids and parents. Invite your friends to come to your house in their pajamas. Have the same kind of party you would have if you were having a sleepover. The only difference is, everyone gets picked up before bedtime. This way, parents are happy to let you join in the fun and friends don't have to worry about sleepover rules!

Here are some fun sleep-under ideas:

1. Have everyone wear their hair in the craziest way they can style it. The craziest wins a prize!
2. Create a scavenger hunt in the house. The winner chooses the movie.
3. Make your own pizzas. Before settling in to watch a movie, use store-bought pizza dough and let everyone choose their own toppings.

4. Play board games or card games. Putting down phones and video games can help you get to know your friends better!

Pizza Party!

Making your own pizza can be really fun. Just be sure to get help from an adult.

Ingredients:
- store-bought (cooked or uncooked) pizza dough
- marinara sauce
- shredded mozzarella cheese
- your choice of pizza toppings, such as pepperoni, sausage, and veggies

Directions:
1. Follow package directions on pizza dough.
2. Spread some marinara sauce evenly over the dough.

3. Put on any toppings you like. Try something new!
4. Sprinkle mozzarella cheese over the toppings and cook the pizza using the directions on the pizza dough package.
5. Eat it up!

Websites to Visit

Find more recipes for sleepover fun:
www.kids-cooking-activities.com

Hairstyle ideas to try at your party:
www.princesshairstyles.com

Get advice about being a good friend:
http://pbskids.org/itsmylife/friends/
index.html

About the Author

Meg Greve writes mostly nonfiction books. In order to write fiction, she had to remember when she was a kid and then change the story to make it more interesting. She played soccer, but never scored a goal, cut her own hair at a sleepover, and had fights with her best friend (but always made up)! Almost all of the story is from her imagination, but some of it has a little bit of truth. Can you guess which parts?

About the Illustrator

Sarah Lawrence always wanted to be an artist, so after graduating from art college in 2006, she took her pencils and started her freelance illustration career. Sarah lives in  Brighton, England, with her daughter, and spends most of her days doodling, drinking tea, and playing princesses.